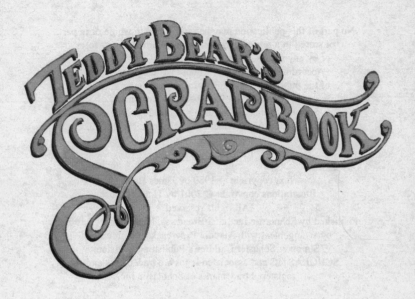

Teddy Bear's Scrapbook

Deborah and James Howe
Illustrated by Timothy Bush

SCHOLASTIC INC.

New York Toronto London Auckland Sydney
Mexico City New Delhi Hong Kong Buenos Aires

With love to Lee Arthur and Lonnelle Howe

ISBN 0-439-37113-9

Text copyright © 1980 by James Howe.
Illustrations copyright © 2001 by Timothy Bush.
All rights reserved.
Published by Scholastic Inc., 555 Broadway, New York, NY 10012,
by arrangement with Aladdin Paperbacks, an imprint of
Simon & Schuster Children's Publishing Division.
SCHOLASTIC and associated logos are trademarks and/or
registered trademarks of Scholastic Inc.

12 11 10 9 8 7 6 5 4   3 4 5 6/0

Printed in the U.S.A.   40

First Scholastic printing, November 2001

Cover design by Debbie Sfetsios

Teddy Bear

CONTENTS

TEDDY BEAR'S SCRAPBOOK

ONE DAY, after it had been raining for a long, long time and I had colored all the pictures in my coloring book, played jacks, dressed my dolls in all their different clothes, read two stories and eaten thirteen cookies, there was NOTHING left to do. It was *that* day that Teddy Bear suggested we look at his scrapbook. Now, I didn't know he even *had* a scrapbook, but, "Oh yes," he said, "I've had this old scrapbook for years. I've just never mentioned it before." He told me it had been in the same trunk in the attic where I had found him that first day we moved into this old house.

"I remember finding you," I said. "What a surprise to open up that old chest and find a teddy bear right on top. You smelled like mothballs!" Teddy giggled. "But I don't remember seeing a scrapbook."

"It was hidden under a blanket," he answered. "I waited until you went to sleep. Then I crept upstairs and sneaked the scrapbook down behind my back. I tiptoed across the floor to your dresser, pulled open your bottom drawer ('cause that was the only one I could reach), and dropped it in. Then I stuck a whole lot of stuff on top of it so you wouldn't notice."

"Why are you going to show it to me now?" I asked.

"Because," he replied, "you need cheering up. You have that 'I'm getting cranky' look, and if you get cranky, I won't have anybody to play with—and that would be no fun at all."

So I walked over to the dresser, opened the bottom drawer, and fished through pajamas and nightgowns until I found it. I pulled out a small, flat, dusty album. The cover was red leather, faded and old-looking, with gold trim around the border and gold lettering in the center that said:

Teddy Bear's Scrapbook

Teddy said, "Hurry up and bring it back to the bed so I can see too. And I'll show you pictures of my life—some of which may surprise you."

I ran to the bed, put Teddy on my lap so we both could see, and opened the album to the first page.

Jackson Hole, WY.

TEDDY ON THE RANGE

"AH YES, this was when I went to Jackson Hole, Wyoming, to work on a ranch."

"Were you really a cowboy?" I asked in amazement.

"Sure. I rounded up cattle and found rustlers, and at night I sat around the campfire with the other cowboys and ate beans."

"Oh my," I said. "I had no idea. Why aren't you a cowboy anymore?"

Teddy was silent for a moment, then he replied softly, "That's a sad story. Are you sure you want to hear it?"

I nodded, and he cleared his throat.

"Well," he began, a faraway look in his eyes, "the rancher had a beautiful daughter—with golden hair as bright as the sun—who loved me very much. I didn't particularly encourage her affection, but you must admit I was a pretty handsome fellow in my cowboy gear."

I had to admit he was, even though his hat made his ears fold over on top of themselves.

"I guess the poor girl couldn't help herself," he went on. Here Teddy sighed deeply, more I think in remembering himself as a dashing young cowboy, than in any fond recollection of the rancher's daughter. "As I say, I went about my business without paying her the slightest bit of attention. Every day I got up at the crack of dawn, said good morning to ol' Nell—"

"Nell? Who's Nell?" I wanted to know.

Teddy pointed to the picture.

"Ah, your horse."

"Yes, my horse. But more than just a horse. Nell was a champion—a one-and-only . . . a . . . a horse's horse!"

"She looks a little swayback to me," I said quietly.

"That may be true," Teddy answered in a way that could have been described as between his teeth if he'd had any, "but that was only because she was old. In her day, she'd been the pride of the stable. When I joined up at the Triple R-Knot Ranch, they were all set to put her out to pasture. But I said, 'No, that's the horse for me.' It was a look in her eye, I guess, a look that said, 'Don't put me out to pasture—not yet—just give me a little more time to run—to feel the free, fresh wind in my mane. . . .'"

I looked at the picture. Nell's eyes sure didn't tell *me* that! If anything, they said, "Take me out to pasture . . . *please!*"

"So Nell and I became fast friends. And as I said, each morning I'd get up, say 'Good morning, Nell,' saddle her up, and we'd be on our way to our round of chores. Checkin' the irrigatin' ditches, ridin' herd, brandin' the new steer with the Triple R-Knot brand, which looked somethin' like this—"

Teddy pointed to the bottom of the page in the scrapbook, and sure enough, there was the Triple R-Knot brand, scorched onto the paper.

"And then after a while, we'd take a checkers and root beer break." Teddy paused and looked down, with a furrowed brow. "Nell always beat me at checkers. I never could figure that out." He looked at me, and I shrugged.

"I guess she just had horse sense," I said.

Teddy looked right through me, as if a response wasn't even worth the bother.

"Then back to work, work, work. Until sunset. And then beans. And then bed. Oh, it was a hard life, all right. Don't be fooled by people tellin' you how glamorous it is to be a cowboy."

"I won't," I promised. "But what about the girl? The rancher's daughter with the hair so bright you could hardly stand to look at it?"

"Oh yes, well, I was coming to her. That all has to do with the rodeo."

"A rodeo?" I shrieked. "Were you in a rodeo?"

"Yes, yes, yes. Now, calm down, or I won't tell you the rest." I calmed down immediately. "Every year the rodeo came to town—the big one, not the little ones like they had every day of the week—but the one with the big stars, and the fancy horses, and all that. And every year, one cowboy from each of the ranches in Jackson Hole got to go and ride in the bronco-bustin' contest. Well, I wasn't givin' it no never-mind. I was just a-standin' there one day, leanin' on the rail of the bunkhouse, mindin' my own business, chewin' on a cheroot, when up sashays the rancher's daughter. And leanin' back beside me, she starts battin' her eyelashes, and she kinda purrs at me. 'Oh, Teddy, are you signin' up for the big rodeo? I just know you could win hands down over all the other cowpokes here. And just think—you could represent the Triple R-Knot and maybe win the trophy for Best Bronco-Buster in the whole of Jackson Hole. And Teddy . . .' and here's where her eyelashes went into overdrive, '. . . my daddy would be so proud of you, I just don't think he'd know what to do.' And she just picked herself up and sashayed right on away. Well, now, I gotta tell you, this started ol' Ted thinkin' in a new direction. Yessum, I gotta tell ya so."

I thought it was kind of cute the way Teddy was leaving all the *g*'s off the ends of his words, and saying things like "Yessum" and "I wasn't givin' it no never-mind," but I was pretty sure it would embarrass him if I pointed it out, so I let him go on.

"Well, I worked hard, I want you to know. Me and Nell, we got up every mornin' long before dawn cracked and went out to the west forty, and I'd tell Nell just to let 'er rip, and I'd try to hold on."

"Oh, Teddy," I said with a smile, "Nell doesn't look like she could throw a Frisbee, let alone a big teddy bear like you."

"Well, sometimes that was true. But then I'd use little tricks. Like one time, I wore my scratchiest wool long johns and she was itchin' so bad, she just couldn't do enough to get me off her back. That was a good workout that day, I'll tell ya. And she was a good horse, Nell was, so she did her best, even when I didn't wear my long underwear. And that pretty lady with the golden hair, she'd come out to watch us sometimes when we worked out in the afternoon. And I have to admit, I started thinkin' how nice lookin' she was, and how makin' her daddy happy wouldn't be the worst thing that could happen to a teddy bear like me. I saw myself lookin' down over that spread of land and saying, 'It's mine, all mine.' And I kinda liked the way that made me feel.

"Well, I guess that line of thinking and all that hard work paid off, because out of all the cowboys there, *I* was chosen to represent the Triple R-Knot in the rodeo. And before you know it, I was signin' up to ride in the bronco-bustin' main event. Oh, and Melissa—that was her name, the rancher's daughter—even made me a special outfit for the Big Day. It was all red and silver and turquoise—oh it was a purty sight, all right. So I rode into town on ol' Nell, who was also all decked out for the occasion. And we waited for the announcement of the main event.

"'Nell,' I whispered, 'this is our big chance. You and me—we're gonna own the Triple R-Knot before you know it, if we just play our cards right. Now, you give it everything you've got. And don't be afraid of hurtin' me. 'Cause what's a little pain? After the cryin's over, we're gonna be on top—yessir!'

"'NEXT EVENT,' the voice thundered over

the loudspeaker, 'BRONCO-BUSTIN'!' AND TO LEAD IT OFF—TEDDY BEAR OF THE TRIPLE R-KNOT RANCH. . . .'

"'This is us, Nell,' I could feel myself start to shake. 'This is us!'

"'TEDDY BEAR WILL BE RIDIN' THE UNCONQUERED, THE UNCONQUERABLE LOCO LOBO—KNOWN THROUGHOUT THE WEST AS THE KILLER!'

"The cheers went up, and my stomach went down—right down to the bottom of my feet. I didn't know I was going to have to ride Loco Lobo. I thought I'd get to ride ol' Nell—just like at home. Nell looked at me. I looked at Nell. And then I looked at Loco Lobo, in the next pen. And I knew it was all over. No one had ever conquered him. One look and I knew why. A tougher, meaner-lookin' critter I'd never seen."

"Poor Teddy!" I exclaimed. "But *you* conquered him, didn't you?"

Teddy didn't answer me. He just got a farther-away look in his eyes, and went on.

"I dropped onto Lobo's back, the gate opened, and we were out. The noise from the crowd was deafening, the sound of it crashing in on me as I was throw into the air, time and again, landing with a force that knocked all the wind out of me. Just when I thought I couldn't take it anymore, an image popped into my mind."

"You, standing on a hilltop, looking down over a spread of land that's yours, all yours?" I asked.

"No, me, lying in a hospital bed with two broken legs and two broken arms. That's when I *knew* I couldn't take it anymore, and I let go. Oh, I went flying! I landed with a great plop!—right in the middle of a big mud puddle. The crowd was booing like crazy, but I thought I still had a chance of winning. 'How long did I last?' I asked the cowpoke who came over to help me up. 'Five minutes? Six? Ten?'

"'Seven seconds.' That's all he said. 'Seven seconds.' A lump came into my throat. I looked down at the mud splattered all over my silver and red and turquoise suit, and when I looked up, I saw Melissa's face, tears running down her cheeks. Even Nell wouldn't speak to me. I knew then and there I no longer had the right to call myself a cowboy. I'd given up the privilege of eating beans around the campfire when I'd landed in the mud."

I sighed a deep sigh. That *was* a sad story. I shook my head as I thought of Teddy falling off that horse.

"What did you do then?" I asked at last.

I thought I saw Teddy wipe a tear from his eye as he answered. "What else could I do? I hung up my gauchos, handed in my dogies, and packed up my troubles. I was out of Jackson Hole before the last rays of sunset disappeared behind the tops of the Teton Mountains. I jumped on the next train headed east, and didn't look back."

"Did you ever hear from Melissa again?"

"No, but Nell wrote me once. She said, 'After everything we went through together, life in the pasture isn't bad at all. Your friend, Nell.' Wasn't that nice?"

"I think so," I said, not at all sure. Teddy looked up at me sadly.

"Come on," I said, giving him a squeeze, "this is exciting. Turn the page. I want to see what's next."

In the Himalayas

A GREAT ADVENTURE!

"IT LOOKS as if you were exploring," I said as soon as I saw the next picture. "Did you go to the North Pole?"

"Far from it. This was actually taken in the Himalayas. I had set out to find the Abominable Snowman."

"The Abominable Snowman! Teddy, weren't you afraid? You didn't go alone, did you? I've always wondered what the

Abominable Snowman was really like, but I don't think I'd try to find out. I'd just take somebody else's word for it. Oh, what a brave thing to do. Did you find him? What was he like? Weren't you scared?"

"You asked me that already," Teddy said, cutting in.

I was so excited I could have asked more and more questions, and poor Teddy would never have had a chance to answer.

"Now, if you'll just listen," he went on, "I'll tell you all about it. But . . ." and here he looked around the room cautiously, ". . . you have to promise to keep this story secret. What I'm about to tell you is just between us."

"Oh, all right," I said, already wondering how I was going to be able not to tell my best friend, Cheryl, who tells me everything and I tell her everything, and we *never* keep secrets from each other. "Go ahead," I said.

"Well," he began, "I had heard about this

creature, the Abominable Snowman, and I decided to find out for myself just who and what he was. All I knew was that he was supposed to be very big and that he lived in the Himalaya Mountains. So one day, I set off loaded up with all my hiking gear and lots of provisions—or so I thought—and most importantly, my camera, in case I got a glimpse of him. Well, the first few days were a piece of cake."

"Is that what you took to eat? That's not very nourishing," I said, trying not to sound like a mother.

"No, that's just an expression. It means that the first few days were easy. I hiked and I hiked, and I rested some, and then hiked some more. No sign of the creature, but I didn't let it worry me. Then, around the fourth day, things started to go wrong. I was now pretty deep into snowy country and my food was running low. I thought I knew where I was headed, but just as I was crossing a ravine, I dropped my compass. Down it went, and with it my only way of knowing which direction to turn."

"You could always use the sun," I suggested.

"Well, that's true, of course. And I did. But then other bad things happened."

"Oh dear."

"You bet 'oh dear.' Shortly after I lost my compass, I twisted my ankle and had to rest for a while. And by then, I was feeling so sorry for myself that I went on an eating binge. I ate everything I had brought with me. Right down to the last drop of honey."

"Oh, Teddy, that wasn't a very smart thing to do." Now I knew I sounded like a mother.

"Of course, it wasn't smart. But I wasn't thinking straight. Too many days out in the sun and snow, I guess. Well, anyway, night fell. I went to sleep, and the next morning when I woke up, I didn't know what to do. I was lost, completely lost. No food, no compass, and my ankle hurt so badly I could hardly move. I just stayed where I was. And before I knew it, I could feel myself falling asleep again. This is it, I thought, good-bye world. And then I didn't think anything else because I was sound asleep."

Teddy stopped for a moment and looked up at me, waiting for a response.

"Well?" he asked, "pretty dramatic, huh? Bet you're wondering how I got out of it alive. Well, I'm going to tell you. But remember, you have to keep this part of it quiet."

"Okay," I whispered, wondering if whispering it to Cheryl would be quiet enough for Teddy.

"When I woke up, I was no longer out in the snow."

"No?"

"No. I was in a very nice cottage, tucked into a *very* big bed. When I opened my eyes, I could see a fire going in the fireplace and a kettle with something that smelled awfully good bubbling away inside it. At first, it was hard to see everything clearly, since there wasn't any light, except from the fire. But it seemed like a place out of a fairy tale, and any minute I expected a little old shoemaker and his little old wife to come hobbling over to the bed and feel my forehead. Instead, I got the shock of my life. The door opened and, with a blast of cold air, in walked a huge teddy bear! I practically jumped out of the bed, except that I didn't have the energy. He looked over at me and said, 'Oh, so you're awake. Would you like some chicken soup? I have some cooking on the fire.'"

"My mouth couldn't even form the words to answer. I just kept staring. He must have been fifteen feet tall, he was kind of a gray color, and his hair was all shaggy. But in a way, he looked very much like me—a regular old teddy bear. Except maybe one with a glandular problem.

"'Don't be afraid,' he went on, 'I won't hurt you. I found you in the snow and brought you here. It was a close call, you know. You had icicles hanging from every part of you. But I got you warmed up in no time. Do you like my home?'

"He seemed to really want to know, so I forced myself to say, 'Yes, v-v-very n-nice.'

"'Oh, good,' he answered, 'I'm glad. I don't have much company here. I'm pleased you like it. Now, how about that chicken soup? It's my own recipe. I know you'll enjoy it. Besides, it's good for you.' Oh, I suppose I should mention that he spoke with an English accent. Naturally, I was curious about that. But now that I'd found my tongue, first things first.

"'Are you the Abominable Snowman?' I asked, as he was ladling up my soup.

"'Well, that's what some people call me. Awful name, don't you think? I do have a name, after all. If they cared to ask, people could call me by my rightful name. What's yours, by the by?'

"'Teddy Bear.'

"'Teddy Bear,' he said back, thinking about it. 'It's a nice name. Simple and direct. I like it. Here, taste this. Tell me if it needs anything.'

"I tasted the soup. It was delicious. It did need a touch of salt, though, and I told him so.

"'Yes, Teddy Bear is a very nice name. American, are you?' I acknowledged that I was. 'Yes, I thought as much. You Americans are so direct, after all. My name's a bit more complicated. But I'm English, you see, and that's the reason for that.' He extended his large, hairy paw. 'Clive Neville-Phillips,' he said. 'Pleased to make your acquaintance.'

"I shook his paw, feeling more at home now, and much better with a little of his chicken soup inside me. 'And a pleasure to meet you, Clive,' I responded, 'but tell me, how is it that you've come all the way to the Himalayas and are known as the Abominable Snowman?'

"'Simple story really. Though, unfortunately, nothing is simple when it involves *people*. I was given as a gift by a family in Mayfair to their rather spoiled little boy on the occasion of his tenth birthday. It seems he didn't want me. Preferred a teddy bear of your size and character to one so, shall we say, grandiose? I suppose I can understand that, really, but what I cannot understand is the abominable—oops, sorry about that— way his parents behaved once he'd rejected me. That very day, they took me to Hampstead Heath and abandoned me. Just like that, one-two-three, out the door and fare-thee-well. I was on my own. Everywhere I went people were frightened of me. I didn't seem to fit in anywhere. So I traveled and traveled, avoiding people as best I could, until I found myself here, in these mountains. A little girl in a village nearby befriended me and has been helping take care of me since. It was she who found this little cottage and set me up here. She's quite delightful. I hope you'll be able to meet her.'

"I said I hoped so too, since I had no idea how to get back and would need a guide."

I interrupted. "How did he survive? That little girl couldn't have paid for his food."

"That's what I wondered," Teddy answered, "so I asked him."

"'Well, that worried me too at first,' he said. 'Naturally, I couldn't depend on this sweet child for everything. But I didn't have a clue as to how to handle the situation.

Then, having a lot of time on my hands, I began to write. After a time, I had a rather respectable collection of short stories—droll, humorous pieces—that I'd written. I sent them off in a bunch to one of England's more important literary magazines. I was quite surprised when they accepted the entire lot! Since then, I've become one of their regular contributors, and in fact, have quite a following. Little do my readers know that their beloved Clive Neville-Phillips is in reality the dreaded Abominable Snowman. You see what I mean when I say it is not really so simple, eh?'

"I certainly had to agree with him about that. Then, feeling drowsy, I drifted back to sleep. I awoke the next day, to see my host and his friend from the village playing dominoes and eating cookies.

"'Have a good sleep?' he asked, ever the thoughtful host. 'Chocolate chip cookie? I made them myself. Quite good, if I do say so.'

"They were indeed. Later that day, I prepared to take my leave. Clive gave me a jar of his chicken soup and a bag of his chocolate chip cookies, and his friend guided me to the village. Before I left, I asked him one favor.

"'I promise not to tell anyone I've actually met you,' I said to him, 'but would it be all right if your friend took a picture of the two of us together? Just for my scrapbook.' Well, he couldn't agree to that. He was very nice about it, but said surely I must appreciate the delicate nature of his situation. Then, after a moment's reflection, he offered a compromise. We stepped outside, and his friend took the picture you see in my scrapbook. That's his footprint I'm standing in."

"Didn't that prove to everyone that you'd found the Abominable Snowman?"

"No, they all thought it was a fake. And I was just as happy, really. After all, Clive had become my friend, and I felt protective toward him. It's just as well that the world has never caught up with him. He lives a happy life in his little cottage, though it must be lonely at times."

"Yes, it must," I agreed. Then I said, "Maybe someday we could go there together and visit him."

"Yes, perhaps we could," Teddy said. "And believe me, it would be well worth the trip. I've never had better chicken soup in my life."

Teddy turned the page.

Clowning Around

TEDDY AT THE CIRCUS

"NOW, HERE'S the one I really like. It brings back such happy memories."

"You were a clown, too?"

"Only for a little while. But in many ways, it was the high point of my life. I loved to make the children laugh. And I made friends with all the people who worked at the circus, and the animals, too—even the lions. Everybody in the circus was happy. It wasn't an easy life, but it was a rewarding one. And I was a *good* clown because my arms and legs are so loose, I could fall down and trip over myself in all sorts of funny ways and never get hurt."

"And besides, you had practice falling when you were a cowboy," I said, teasing. Teddy frowned at me, and I behaved.

"But, of course, my greatest adventure was not as a clown at all," he continued. "It was the day I walked the high wire."

"You didn't!" I gasped.

"I had to," he answered, "there was a damsel in distress."

He sounded so grand when he said that. I had always wanted to be a damsel in distress, even though I wasn't quite sure what it was.

"At one performance, the high-wire artist, a beautiful lady with golden curls, slipped when she was halfway across the wire and was suddenly hanging on by one hand. She'd been sick with measles the whole week before, and everyone told her not to go on that day, but she thought only of all those people who had paid to see her, and she said, 'I must go on!' And so she did." Teddy stopped for a moment and leaned back on one elbow.

"You know, people think there's nothing to being a clown. They think it's easy, that all you have to do is go out there and make silly faces and fall down a lot. But there's more to it than that. Why, I had to study for a long time to be a clown. I'll bet you didn't know that clowns have to study, did you?"

I had to admit I didn't. I wanted to ask Teddy to get back to the story, but he seemed determined to tell me how hard it was to be a clown. He got a stern look on his face, the kind my dad gets when he's about to tell me something for my own good. Like when he says: "Do you have any idea what it was like when *I* was *your* age, young lady?" Boy, I knew dads were like that, but I sure didn't expect it from my teddy bear.

Teddy cleared his throat, and I looked down at him. He must have been reading my mind, because he sat up and said, "Well, I guess you don't really want to hear about all that, anyway. Where was I?"

"The high-wire lady," I said, relieved.

"Oh yes, Miranda. Well, it was—do you have any idea what kind of condition you have to be in to take all those falls? You have to know *how* to fall. If you're all tense, it's no good. You'll just hurt yourself."

"Oh. Uh-huh. I'll remember that." I tried to avoid looking in his eyes. There was a pause while he waited for me to say something else. Finally, he spoke.

"What was I saying?"

"Melissa."

"Who?"

"Melissa, the high-wire lady."

"Oh, you mean Miranda. Melissa was the rancher's daughter."

"Oh yes. I'm sorry. Miranda."

"That's hard work too, walking the tightrope. Everybody thinks it just takes nerves. And it does take nerves, but it takes a lot of work, too. You have to practice, practice, practice. Takes skill, I'll tell you that. Nerve and skill. Nerve and skill and practice. Um-hmmm." He paused, and I thought he was finished. But then he said, "Nerve and skill and practice, practice, practice!"

"Teddy!" I was ready to jump out of my skin. "Will you *please* tell me the rest of the story?!"

"Oh yes. Sorry. Well, as I told you, Miranda had been sick. But she went on, anyway. And then, when she was halfway across the wire, down she went, until she was hanging on with one hand. When I saw her fall, I didn't even stop to think about my own safety. I practically flew up the long ladder and stepped out onto the wire without a moment's hesitation. It was only after I'd taken a few steps that I realized where I was."

"What did you do?" I asked breathlessly.

"I made a *very big mistake*. I looked down. My head started swimming, and the next thing I knew, *I* slipped, too! Somehow my knee caught on the wire, so that I was hanging upside down. The crowd gasped. Then there wasn't a sound. And then, while I tried to get back to the wire, I heard someone laughing. One little laugh. Far away. And then someone else. And then someone else. And more and more laughs, until my ears were ringing with the sound of people laughing. I don't know how I did it, but I managed to get to my feet again, walk a few inches, and then *down* I went again, this time catching the wire with both hands. Well, the audience loved that one. They laughed even harder than the first time. And then I realized they thought I was doing it on purpose! After all, I *was* a clown. Little did they know that I was scared out of my wits. And poor Miranda—I saw the look on her face. *She* knew I wasn't kidding around. Hand over hand, I inched my way to her until we were looking into each other's faces.

"'What do we do now?' she asked me. I told her to put her arms around my neck, and I'd take her to safety. Thank goodness she didn't weigh very much. Because hanging from the wire like that, I couldn't take too much of an extra load. When we got to the end of the wire, she stepped up onto my shoulders and then onto the platform—and safety. Then she took my hands and helped me up. There was a thunderous burst of applause from the audience as we turned and waved. I broke into a big smile. (I couldn't help myself.) And then I fainted."

"Oh, you poor thing," I said, cuddling him.

"But it was all right. I woke up, my head in the beautiful lady's lap, and when we got to the ground, she gave me a big kiss."

I didn't like that part, but I didn't say anything.

Teddy turned the page. "See this? This was the headline in the next day's paper."

TEDDY BEAR SAVES THE DAY
VALIANT CLOWN RISKS LIFE FOR BEAUTIFUL HIGH-WIRE ARTISTE!

I looked at Teddy as he gazed at the headline, his button-eyes shining with pride. He turned to me and with a sigh, said, "They thought it was all part of the act—that I was just a clown up there. But when they found out the truth—I was a hero! Oh, those were great days, and that was the greatest of them all. But as with all good things . . ."

"It had to end?" I asked. "But why?"

"One of the lions forgot we were friends and tried to eat me for lunch. I didn't care for that. So I moved on."

"I don't blame you," I said. "I don't think I would care for it either." I turned the page.

More than a cub reporter

TEDDY: ACE REPORTER

"OH," I CRIED in disappointment before I could stop myself, "this one doesn't look very interesting."

"Are you kidding?" Teddy asked seriously. "This was one of the most exciting and dangerous episodes of my life. I was the ace crime reporter for the *Chicago Daily News*."

"What does that mean?" I asked. "It

looks as if you just had to write a lot of things down in a notebook."

"Listen, sweetheart," Teddy said in a tone of voice I'd never heard him use before, "you'd whistle a different tune if you'd ever walked that Southside beat. I had to have the soles of my feet resewn after a few months on that job. I'd been put on a case that nobody else had been able to crack. The best detectives on the force couldn't make head nor tail of it, and six reporters before me had come in empty-handed. That's when the boss called me in and said, 'Ted, I'm going to put you on the toughest case I've ever seen—the Case of the Missing Milk Money. We've had a few leads, but they all end up nowhere. All we know is that hundreds of Chicago schoolchildren are being robbed of their precious milk money. We don't know who's behind it—and neither do the police. Here's a chance for a big scoop, kid. Go to it.'"

"Teddy," I interrupted, "did you solve the mystery all by yourself?"

"You don't get to be an ace reporter by following the crowd, kid. I had to go it alone, notebook in hand, all my senses at the ready."

"How did you do it?"

"Well, the first step is to use a little psychology. You know what that means?"

I shook my head. I hated it when Teddy used big words I didn't understand.

"It has to do with the way people behave—what makes them do the things they do," he explained. "I had to try to figure out just what kind of person would steal milk money from schoolchildren."

"Not a very nice one," I said. That much psychology even I knew.

"No, not a very nice one. But what else could we say about him? Or her? I didn't have a clue to go on. My hunches told me that this person hated milk! But why would that make him steal milk money from kids?"

I looked blankly at Teddy. This was a real mystery, and I didn't know what to say. Finally, Teddy broke the silence.

"That's what *I* thought at first, too. *Nothing.* Then I started reading up. I read some Freud, and that cleared the whole thing up for me. Now this Freud character—he's a big deal in psychology, see—he says that everything we do when we're grown up is because of something that happened to us when we were kids. So I decided this thief probably had a mother who made him drink so much milk he couldn't stand it anymore, and now he was going to make it so that if he had *his* way, no little kid would have to drink any milk at all—ever again!"

"But that's terrible," I cried. "*I* like milk. Lots of kids like milk. He shouldn't be allowed to do that."

"Of course, he shouldn't," Teddy answered.

"And that's where I came in. I was going to put a stop to it. Now that I had his personality figured out, I had to find out how he did what he did. In order to do that, I'd need a disguise. That way I could fit into the scene without his ever suspecting a thing, get it?" Teddy winked at me.

"Disguises were sort of my trademark. Once I dressed up as a butler in a murder case. The only thing was it turned out the butler did it! Boy, I had a fine time getting out of that mess. But this time I was stumped just coming up with a disguise. I didn't know *what* I was going to do. I decided I really looked too old to pass myself off as a student. So I thought some more. I thought and I thought—and then it came to me in a flash. It was simple, really. I couldn't believe it hadn't occurred to me sooner. You see, kiddo, I looked at it this way: take off the raincoat and hat, and what have you got?"

"A teddy bear," I said.

"Precisely. And what could be a better disguise? All I had to do was get out of my detective duds, climb up onto one of the shelves in the classroom and pretend to be a *toy*! Clever, huh? That way I could see and hear everything that went on. And no one would suspect a thing."

"How did it feel to be a teddy bear?" I asked.

Teddy shrugged. "It's okay. No big thing. I must admit it was nice change of pace for a while. Nice and quiet."

"Did anything happen?"

"Well, nothing to do with our thief at first. Of course, a few kids tried to play with me, but I just told them to buzz off. And after that, they left me alone so I could go about my business. Then, finally, after almost a week of waiting . . . the payoff! One Friday morning, all the kids came in crying to their teacher—some mean man had stopped them on their way into school and demanded their milk money. I listened long enough to find out the location of the scene of the crime—and took off in a flash. I got to the street corner, looked around and didn't see our man. But then I noticed a little candy store, and I thought to myself, Aha, where would this kind of lowdown character who hates milk go after he's made off with all that money? Why, what better place than the candy store to fill up on soda pop."

"Oh, that's very clever," I said.

"Basic Freud," Teddy replied. "He was getting even with his mother. I grabbed a cop who was standing nearby and together we burst into the store. Sure enough, there he was—drinking down what looked like his third bottle of soda. 'Okay, officer,' I said, 'do your duty. This is the creep who's been stealing milk money from all those helpless little children.'"

"Who was it?" I asked.

"Shorty 'the Slug' Loomis, a tough cookie if ever there was one. It was a real feather in my cap to bring him down, I'll tell you. He was one of the Ten Most Wanted Criminals in Chicago."

"You mean he did more than steal milk money?"

"Oh yeah, that was small stuff for the Slug."

"Gee, he must have really hated milk."

"He did."

"Chocolate, too?"

"Yep, even chocolate. Oh, here's the headline in the next day's paper. *My* story—Column One, Page One."

MILK MONEY MOBSTER PEGGED AS PILFERER OF PUPILS' PENNIES

BY Teddy Bear, Ace Reporter

"My, you certainly have a way with words."

Teddy nodded his head. "Thanks, kid. It was nice getting a big story like that. But after the story broke, I got a little scared. I started getting empty milk cartons in the mail. Not a good sign, I thought. The Slug was really burned up about the whole thing. I'll never forget his last words to me, as I left the courtroom: 'I'll get you for this, Bear. Your days are numbered in this town.' So what else could I do?"

I shook my head.

"I left town, of course."

"Of course." And I turned the page.

Halloween at Chez Mimi

WHITE ALL OVER

"OH!" I exclaimed when I saw the next picture. "What happened here?"

"I was baking a cake that day," Teddy said with a chuckle, "but something went wrong."

"So you were a baker, too?" I asked, thinking by now that Teddy had been and done just about everything!

"I was more than a baker," he answered,

ready to tell me his story. "I was a chef. You know what a chef is, don't you?"

"Sure, it's like a cook—only fancier."

"That's right. I was the fanciest cook for the fanciest restaurant in town: *Chez Mimi.* Now, Mimi was a beautiful lady . . . and kind—"

"Did she have golden hair?"

"Hmm, let me think. Why, yes, as a matter of fact, she did. Why do you ask?"

"Oh, never mind. Go ahead, tell your story."

"It was the most important night of the year at *Chez Mimi:* Halloween—when the biggest names in society came to our restaurant in all sorts of costumes for an evening of fun and food. Even the staff was encouraged to dress up—but I'd been so busy preparing the evening's meal, I'd forgotten to get a costume. I was very upset, because I really had my heart set on winning the first-prize ribbon for Best Costume. But, my cooking had to come first, and I was so far behind with the preparations that I still hadn't begun the cake when the guests started to arrive. I had to work as fast as I could. Everything went flying—eggs, milk, nuts, butter, honey. Well, I was going to put in some honey, but I couldn't help myself— I ate the whole jar, so there wasn't any left for the cake!

"Finally, it was time to add the flour to the batter. I had to climb up on the shelf and pull myself to the top of a very tall tin that held the flour and—remember I said I was in a hurry—I guess I just didn't take time to balance properly, so *in* I went, head over feet, right into the tin of flour. Luckily, my friend, Milton the Penguin, came in the door just then."

I looked at the second picture on the page. "Is this Milton?" I asked.

Milton

"Yes, he was the headwaiter. Of course, he didn't always look like that. That night, he was dressed as a pirate. Made him look silly, if you ask me. Whoever heard of a pirate penguin? Anyway, Milton came in and called out my name. I poked my head over the top of the tin and yelled, 'Here I am! Help me get out of here!'"

"'Teddy, is that you?' he asked. 'What a terrific costume!'

"'What costume?'

"'That polar bear suit you've got on. It's great.'

"Well, of course I had to smile because I hadn't planned it at all. But I wasn't going to let Milton know that. 'Oh, it's just something I threw together,' I said. 'Glad you like it.' Just then, some flour got up my nose and I sneezed. A big cloud of flour exploded around me. Milton helped me get out of the tin and together we finished the cake."

"How was it?"

"Scrumptuous! It was the hit of the evening. But the best part was when Milton and I came out of the kitchen carrying the cake. All eyes turned toward us. Mimi came running over to me and kissed me on the cheek. 'Ah, *mon cher*,' she cried. That means 'my dear' in French—"

"I *know*," I said dryly. I didn't really, but I felt it was time to put Teddy in his place.

"'Ah, *mon cher*,' she cried, 'what an inspired creation!' I thought she meant the cake, but it was my 'costume' she was talking about. 'You win First Prize! Teddy the Polar Bear! What a clever one you are,' and kissed me again."

"Yick," I said, "don't you get tired of all those ladies kissing you?"

"Do you get tired of eating cookies?"

"Well, no—"

"Well, I don't get tired of being kissed."

I wasn't sure I understood that, but Teddy had already turned the page.

"Here, look," he said.

Awarded to Teddy

Bear—

Costumed as a

Polar Bear!

I had to smile. "Oh, Teddy," I giggled, "you really are a clever one."

"I know," he answered, "and a great chef, too!"

The next picture took me completely by surprise.

A big BIG star

TEDDY IN HOLLYWOOD

"A MOVIE STAR! I never saw any of your movies."

"Oh, it was many years ago."

"But I never saw them on the late, late show either."

"Maybe that's because you're not allowed to stay up that late. Or then again, maybe it's because I made only one picture, and I think that one's been lost."

"Did many people see it?" I asked.

"It was a smash," he said. "Even got me an Academy Award nomination."

"Did you win?"

"No, they gave it to Lassie! As if a dog could act."

I didn't say anything more about that. I thought it best not to. After all these years, Teddy still seemed bitter about losing an Oscar to a dog.

"Well, never mind. Those were good times, anyway," Teddy continued after a moment. "Here I am with a few of my close friends. Ah yes, glamour, money, fame . . . it was good while it lasted."

I turned the page. Teddy was on the cover of a magazine.

"I don't know why anybody would want to leave such a wonderful life. Look, you're even on a magazine cover," I looked at Teddy in a new way—I'd never known anyone who had been on the cover of a magazine, except my friend, Cheryl, who was once on the cover of the Hillsdale Elementary School PTA Report dressed as a frog. "Don't tell me you had to leave Hollywood, too."

"Well, not quite," Teddy said, "but let

me tell you, baby, Hollywood is no bed of roses. It's a town with a silver dollar where its heart should be. After *It Happened One Nut,* I started working on *Teddy Bears on Parade.* What a great movie that was going to be! All singing, all dancing, fifty laughs every five minutes. One hundred dancing teddy bears! And girls! What beauties!"

"Teddy," I said, "I don't want to hear about the girls." I didn't tell him, but I was beginning to feel a little jealous. Teddy had lived such a glamorous life, and everywhere there seemed to be girls, girls, girls.

"Well, it doesn't matter anyway," he answered. "The movie was never finished. For weeks, we shot out in the back lot. One day, while I was working on the big dance number with my director, Buzzy Bunny, I was paged on the set."

"What does that mean?" I asked.

"It means someone was looking for me."

"Not Shorty 'the Slug' Loomis!" I cried.

"Nah, he was servin' twenty in San Quentin then. He didn't worry me. Besides, he was probably one of my biggest fans. Everybody loved me in those days."

"So who was looking for you?"

"Melinda, my childhood sweetheart. She'd come all the way to Hollywood just to ask me to come home."

I was disappointed. Another woman in Teddy's life. This time I really got mad.

"Well, I certainly hope you didn't go!" I snapped. "Why should you leave Hollywood just for some childhood sweetheart?"

"That's what *I* said," Teddy answered. "Why, I practically laughed in her face. *Me,* go back home, when all America is waiting for the next Teddy Bear picture, and the next and the next? No thanks, that's what I told her. I'm riding a rainbow and I'm not coming down. She looked very sad then, and I felt kind of sorry I'd said it, but that's how I saw things in those days. She walked away without saying another word, and I went back to my trailer, put on my tap shoes and reported to the set. We were working on a terrific number: 'We're in the Honey!'"

"Do you remember any of it?" I asked. "Can you sing it?"

Teddy jumped down from the bed, as if he'd just been waiting for me to ask and began to dance and sing his way across the floor. He was really very good! He sang:

> "Oh, we are just a bunch of bears
> Looking for fortune and fame
> Came all the way from Iowa
> 'Cause Broadway's the name of the game.
>
> Now it's almost opening night
> And our hearts are all a-patter
> As we see our names go up in lights

And our bankrolls growing fatter . . .

Oh, we're in the honey
We're in the honey
Everything in life is so sweet
Just can't stop our dancin' feet
'Cause we're in the honey now!"

Teddy ended with a great flourish, and I clapped my hands happily. "That was wonderful!"

"Well, it's been a few years," he said modestly. "You should have seen me then. Besides, I don't have my tap shoes. Boy, could this bear tap."

"So, what happened? Why didn't the film ever get made?"

"Wouldn't you know it? Just as we were going into our last day of shooting, word got out that another studio was releasing *Collies on Parade* in just two weeks. Starring guess who?"

I didn't have to guess. I could see it in Teddy's eyes.

"Lassie, the wonder-dog, winner of the Academy Award. Suddenly, everybody loved collies and nobody loved teddy bears. Our picture was canceled, and *Collies on Parade* became a big hit. After that, nobody wanted to hear from T. Bear anymore. I was just another has-been."

"What about the other pictures you were going to do?"

"Canceled. All canceled," he replied. "I worked for a while washing dishes in Rosie's Diner at Hollywood and Vine, but then even Rosie didn't want me. She said I was hurting the image of the place. I thought it was all over. Nobody loved me. Nobody wanted me. One day I was America's favorite, the next day I wasn't good enough to scrape plates at Rosie's. I was walking along the beach one night, thinking . . . it wouldn't make much difference to anybody . . . if I just—"

"No, Teddy!"

"Yes. But then I remembered. A girl with golden hair, who had said, 'Come home, Teddy.' With my last dime, I called—collect, of course—and Melinda said, 'I miss you, Teddy, we all do. Come home. You're still the most important bear in the whole world to us.' And so I left Hollywood. And I came home."

"I'll bet you miss it sometimes though, don't you? The parties, the excitement of making movies . . ."

"Oh, once in a while, a little bit. But then I just open up my scrapbook and remember . . . and that's enough."

He turned the page one more time.

Home with Melinda

TEDDY & MELINDA

"WHAT ARE YOU in this picture?" I asked, after looking at it for a minute.

"Why, I'm a teddy bear, of course," he replied.

I noticed that the girl in the picture had golden curls, just like the girls in Teddy's stories. And her name was Melinda, just like the girl who brought him home from Hollywood. I was getting worried. I wasn't sure I really wanted to know about this story, but I *was* curious, so I asked, "Where was this picture taken?"

"Right here in this house. In fact, in this room."

I looked around my room. That picture was taken *here*? "But it doesn't look anything like this room."

"That's because it was taken many years ago."

"How many?"

"Oh, I don't know. Thirty or forty."

I couldn't even imagine how many years thirty or forty were. Suddenly, Teddy seemed very old, and I felt very young. Now I wanted to know about Melinda.

"Teddy?" I asked. Teddy's eyes were still fixed on the picture.

"Mmmm?"

"Who was this girl? Who was Melinda?"

Teddy looked up at me. "Melinda was

like you, in a way," he answered. "She was the first little girl to own me. I was given to her as a Christmas present in . . . oh, nineteen thirty-four, I guess it was . . . and I lived with her here in this room until about nineteen forty-six . . . yes, that's right . . . twelve years."

"Then what happened?"

"She grew up. I was put in a trunk in the attic, together with my scrapbook. The family moved away and left me there. And there I've been—until you came along and found me." I was very sad, thinking of Teddy up in the attic all that time.

"Did you love Melinda very much?"

"She was the love of my life," he answered simply.

I was sorry I had asked. I closed the scrapbook and sat for a long moment without moving. At last, Teddy tapped me on the arm.

"A penny for your thoughts," he whispered.

I didn't speak right away. Then I said, softly, "I wish *I* were the love of your life. But I don't even have golden curls. I have flat brown hair."

Teddy broke out laughing. "I *love* flat brown hair," he said, "and you *are* the love of my life."

"But you said—"

"I said Melinda *was* the love of my life. But that was then. She loved me when I was new and I didn't have a patch on my leg and my buttons were shiny and bright. But you love me when I'm old and maybe just a little shabby. And that's an even greater love: to love somebody when he's a little old and worn at the edges."

I gave Teddy a big squeeze. "But you're even better now that you are old. So many exciting things have happened to you. You wouldn't have had any stories to tell me when you were brand-new. I'll love you always," I cried. "I'll never, ever put you away in a trunk."

I started to get down from the bed to put the scrapbook away when Teddy stopped me.

"Wait a minute," he said, "there's one more page."

"But it's blank," I said, turning to the last page of the scrapbook.

"It is now," Teddy said, "but it doesn't have to stay that way." And he picked up a crayon and wrote in big, big letters at the bottom of the page:

BEST FRIENDS!

And now when you come to my house, I'll show you Teddy Bear's scrapbook, and on the last page, this is what you'll see:

Teddy and me!

BEST FRIENDS!